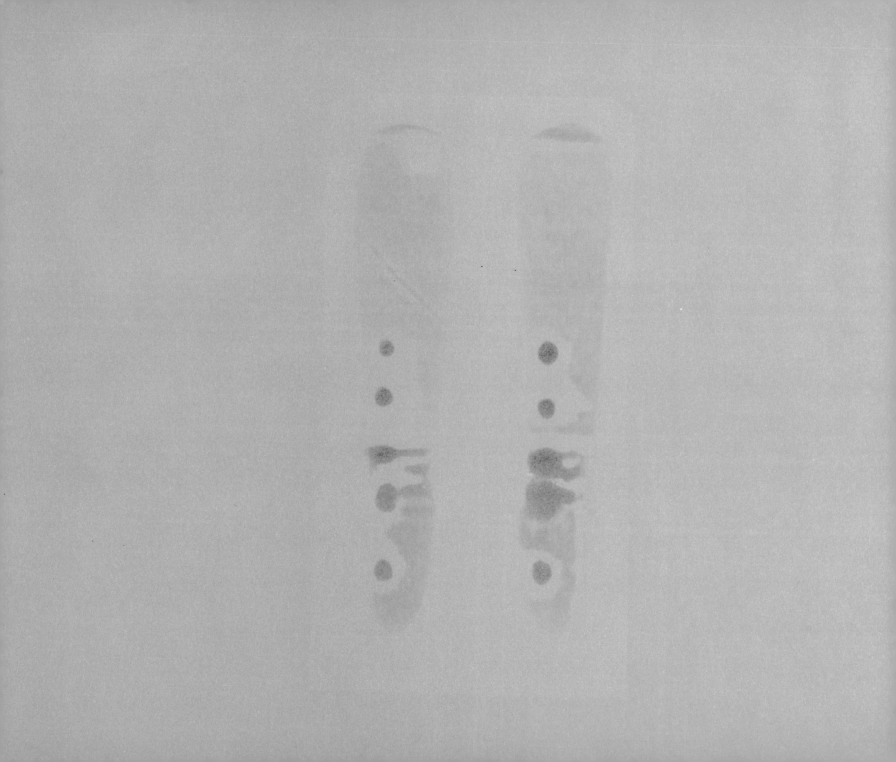

In My Mother's Garden

by Melissa Madenski

Illustrated by Sandra Speidel

Little, Brown and Company

Boston New York Toronto London

First Edition

Library of Congress Cataloging-in-Publication Data

Melissa, Madenski.
  In my mother's garden / by Melissa Madenski ; illustrated by Sandra Speidel. — 1st ed.
    p. cm.
  Summary: With the help of a neighbor, a young girl plants some pansies as a birthday surprise for her mother.
  ISBN 0-316-54326-8
  [1. Gardening — Fiction. 2. Birthdays — Fiction. 3. Mothers and daughters — Fiction.] I. Speidel, Sandra, ill. II. Title.
PZ7.M256475In 1995
[E] — dc20   93-40112

10 9 8 7 6 5 4 3 2 1

NIL

Published simultaneously in Canada by Little, Brown & Company (Canada) Limited

Printed in Italy

On the first day of spring, I sit up in bed and look out my window. I slide my fingers around in a circle on the foggy glass and look at the garden. Flower stalks from last year's plants look like marching soldiers with stiff arms and legs. I watch Mom cut back her favorite rosebush so it will have more flowers when it blooms. She wants to pick roses for bouquets every day this summer. I tap on the window, and she looks up at me and waves.

I pull the blankets up around my shoulders and hug myself. Today our neighbor Joe is taking me to the flower nursery to help me plan a birthday surprise for Mom. I'm going to build her a little garden of pansies, her favorite flowers.

"Rosie," my mother calls up the stairs, "come get some breakfast —
Joe will be here soon."

I slide into my chair at the table, but I'm so excited I can't sit
still.

"I bet you can't wait to ride a two-wheeler," says Mom.

"Joe said he'd take the training wheels off this morning," I tell
her.

This is the first big secret I've ever kept. I'm so afraid I might tell
her what we're really doing that, between bites of cereal, I put my
hand over my mouth to hold in the surprise.

"Do you feel sick, Rosie?" Mom asks.

"No, just excited," I tell her.

After breakfast, I go outside and get my bike ready to put in Joe's truck. The driveway is bumpy, and I have to grab the handlebars tight so the bike won't tip over.

Joe comes up the driveway in his big red truck, so I leave my bike in the grass and run to meet him. I try to beat my brother, Nathan, who is racing to Joe's truck from the house. I get to Joe first, and he swings me high above his head. "Pretty soon, Rosie," he tells me, "you'll be too big for an old guy like me to lift up." Nathan grabs him around the waist. We walk up to the house, Nathan still holding on to Joe, and me riding on his shoulders.

Mom and Joe sit on the porch and talk about their gardens.

"Rosie helped me start the tomato seeds inside last week," Mom tells Joe.

"She's gettin' to be a real little gardener," Joe says, smiling.

"When Rosie and the garden were small," says Mom, "I used to pay Nathan a quarter to make sure she didn't eat dirt." She tells Joe how Nathan would sit me on the lawn next to the garden paths. "He'd fill his dump truck with rocks and unload them next to her. He'd say in a very loud voice, 'Don't you eat those, now, Rosie.'"

"Yuck," I say, "I can't believe I ate dirt."

"You ate so much dirt," says Mom, "I thought I could probably sprout seeds if I just laid them on your arms."

I look at my arms and think of plants growing around my hands and fingers.

Joe gets up and puts out his hand to pull me up. "We've got some serious bike riding to do, Rosie." We climb into the cab of the truck and laugh about our surprise.

As we bounce over the gravel road and out onto the highway, I think about how I will keep the garden a secret until Mom's birthday. Joe and I don't say much. Joe sings a song or two, and I sing along when I know the words.

The nursery, with yellow, red, and purple flowers next to the front door, looks like a picture book. Joe rides me around in a big green cart. He hums as he picks out forget-me-nots as blue as a summer sky. He drives the cart around the back of the greenhouse, where they keep the pansies. Rows and rows of purple-and-white flowers look like the biggest bouquet I've ever seen.

I jump out of the cart and pull Joe over to smell the blossoms. "Mom told me once she'd like a field of pansies in the spring so she'd know that summer was almost here," I tell him.

"Well, her wish just came true," says Joe. We load the cart with pots of pansies. I think of how Mom will look when she sees her surprise. She'll probably say, "This is the best present ever," or she might say, "You always know what I like, Rosie," or even "Rosie, you've made me so happy, I don't know what to say."

On the way home, I hold one of the pansy plants in my lap. My fingers dig through the dirt like burrowing earthworms. The flowers smell sweet, and I close my eyes and think of hot sunny days in my mother's garden. I think of how Mom pops warm ripe berries into my mouth as we fill our buckets after summer picnics.

Joe and I stop at the café for ice cream. I get strawberry and Joe gets vanilla so we can trade bites.

The ice cream makes my hands cold. When I'm done, I stick them in my pockets.

"When you were born," Joe tells me, "your mom put in a garden just for you. And it seems as if with each year you grow, she adds another little space of dirt for some more flowers."

"She says gardening clears her head," I tell him.

"Well, now you're gonna get a chance to clear yours." He laughs and gives me a poke on the arm.

Joe promises to come over Sunday. "You look for the perfect spot," he says.

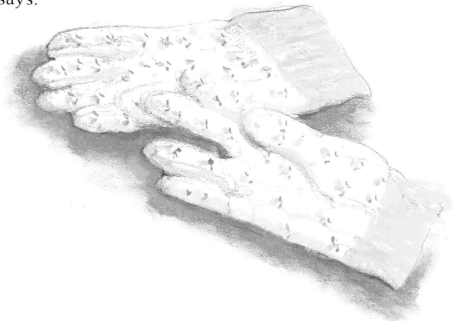

Joe's wife, Karen, calls that night and asks Mom to go to the nursery on Sunday.

"Rosie," Mom calls to me, "do you want to go, too?"

I tell her I have to practice my bike with Joe.

"You must be getting very good at riding." She laughs.

"No skinned knees yet," I say.

On Sunday, I listen to my brother read the funnies aloud, but all the time I'm thinking about Mom's surprise.

Joe drives Karen over, and Mom and Nathan climb into the truck. Joe puts me on his shoulders. I tell him to walk down by the blackberry bushes, where Mom never goes. Last night, while Mom made dinner, I raked the leaves and weeds off a spot as big as the garden cart we used to haul the pansies. The spot is just a big brown square, but when I look at it, I see all the flowers that will grow there.

In the toolshed, I take out two shovels, and a little lime in a bucket. Mom says almost every plant likes a little bit of room and a little bit of lime around its roots. I tuck my gardening gloves into my sweatshirt pocket. They're soft inside with roses printed on the outside. Mom bought them for me last spring. "If you're old enough to help me as much as you do," she said, "you're old enough to have your own gloves."

I put a leaf where I want each plant to go, just the way Mom taught me. Joe and I dig twelve holes, one for each pansy. A few earthworms stretch into my holes, and I put them under the ferns.

Sometimes Mom talks to her flowers, so I say, "Grow well, little plants," as I pat the soil around the pansies with the palms of my hands.

Even though I'm covered with dirt, I feel clean, as if I just had a swim in the creek. Maybe that's what Mom means when she talks about clearing her head.

During the next few weeks, I sneak down at suppertime to watch the pansies. In a few days, it will be Mom's birthday.

"When am I going to get to see you on that two-wheeler?" Mom asks me one night at dinner.

"Maybe by your birthday," I tell her.

I smile at my brother, who thinks I can't keep anything secret.

The day before Mom's birthday, I race down to check the pansies. They smell sweet and have grown since Joe and I put them in the ground. A big earthworm wiggles under the plants, where it is cool and dark.

On Mom's birthday, I get up before anyone else. The house is cold. I get dressed quickly and run out to the birthday garden and pick a pansy. I bang the screen door behind me because I can't wait for Mom to get up. I run up to her room and lay the flower on her pillow.

"Rosie, how sweet," she says. "You know how much I love pansies."

I grab Mom's hand and pull her out of bed. "Come with me," I tell her.

"Can't I get dressed?" she asks.

I hand her a big sweater and pull her toward the stairs.

"OK," she says, laughing, "but I think on my birthday, I'm supposed to be able to do what I want."

"You'll want to do this," I say.

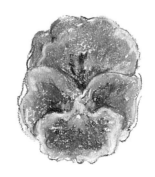

I take her outside to the front porch. The garden is shiny, and the spiderwebs are like bridges between the rosebushes.

I hop off the steps and do a little dance in front of Mom.

"Guess what I am," I say.

"A bird," guesses Mom.

"No-o-o-o," I answer.

"A ballerina," she guesses again.

"No-o-o-o," I say. "Do you give up?"

"Yes," Mom says, "I give up."

"Well, come with me, and I'll tell you." We walk down to the birthday garden. Mom holds my hand and gives it a squeeze.

At the garden I say, "I'm a little purple pansy, of course," and I show Mom how the young flowers start all curled up and then open to face the sun.

Mom looks very happy. She sits down beside the garden and lightly touches the flowers. Then she pulls me on her lap and gives me a big hug. "This is the best birthday surprise I've ever had."

"I thought you'd say that," I tell her.

"And," she says, "the prettiest flower in my garden is sitting right here in my lap."

We laugh, and I jump up to show her the pansy dance again.
"I'm not just any flower," I tell her. "I'm a little purple pansy —
of course."